For Tom, Diana, Alex and Amy
with lots of love from Embo xxx

Bloomsbury Publishing, London, Oxford, New York, New Delhi and Sydney

First published in Great Britain in 2018 by Bloomsbury Publishing Plc
50 Bedford Square, London WC1B 3DP

www.bloomsbury.com

BLOOMSBURY is a registered trademark of Bloomsbury Publishing Plc

Text and illustrations copyright © Emily MacKenzie 2018
The moral rights of the author/illustrator have been asserted

A CIP catalogue record of this book is available from the British Library

ISBN 978 1 4088 7400 4 (HB)
ISBN 978 1 4088 8296 2 (PB)
ISBN 978 1 4088 8294 8 (eBook)

All papers used by Bloomsbury Publishing are natural, recyclable products made
from wood grown in well managed forests. The manufacturing processes
conform to the environmental regulations of the country of origin

Printed in China by Leo Paper Products, Heshan, Guangdong
1 3 5 7 9 10 8 6 4 2

Eric Makes a SPLASH

Emily MacKenzie

BLOOMSBURY

LONDON OXFORD NEW YORK NEW DELHI SYDNEY

Eric was a **worrier**.

He **worried** about **noises** in the **night**.

He **worried** about finding **spiders** in his **welly boots**.

He **worried** about getting **lost** at the **park**.

But nothing worried Eric more than . . .

"no thanks."

"hmmm . . ."

. . . trying NEW things.

"eek!"

Luckily Eric had a **brave** and **kind** best friend
who **loved** to help him feel **brave** too.

Flora was **fearless** and Eric thought she was just **wonderful!**

On Monday Flora wanted to **splash** in **muddy puddles** but Eric worried about getting his boots dirty.

"Why don't you pretend you're a **piglet** rolling in mud or a **hippo** having a bath?" suggested Flora.

Soon they were

sploshing

and

splashing

together.

On Tuesday Eric worried that he wouldn't like the new sandwich filling his mum had put in his packed lunch.

"Why don't you pretend you're a **bear**, Eric?" said Flora.

"Bears **love** honey and they are big, strong and very fuzzy wuzzy. I bet it tastes yummy!"

Eric wasn't sure, but he had a bite . . .

. . . and Flora was right –
honey WAS delicious!

On Wednesday Eric worried that the **VERY TALL** climbing frame was making his knees wobbly.

"Why don't you pretend you're a **spider** on a **giant** sticky web," said Flora. "Then you won't fall off!"

And on Thursday Eric was worried about the scary dark.

"Let's pretend we're **owls,** Eric!" said Flora.
"They fly at night all the time!"

Together they
hooted
and
twit-twooed
loudly.

But on Friday something arrived in the post
that made Eric **very** worried indeed . . .

It was an invitation to a swimming party.

IT'S GOING TO BE SPLISHY!

IT'S GOING TO BE SPLASHY!

Dear: **ERIC**

You are invited to:

DESMOND AND RAYMOND'S SWIMMING PARTY!

Time: **2 PM SATURDAY**

Where: **SOGGY TOWEL SWIMMING POOL**

See you there! Don't forget your towel!

This sent Eric into a worrying whirl.

What if his **fur** got wet?

What if water went in his **eyes**?

What if he **sank** to the **bottom** of the **pool**?

"Why don't we go shopping and buy you some new swimming trunks?" said Flora.

But even Eric's favourite pair didn't make him feel any better.

"Ta-dah!" said Flora. "Look! A swimming cap with a **dinosaur** on it. This will keep your fur dry.

And how about these goggles?"

But Eric **still** worried. Until . . .

"Now we're getting somewhere!"
said Eric with a smile.

Finally they were off to the pool.

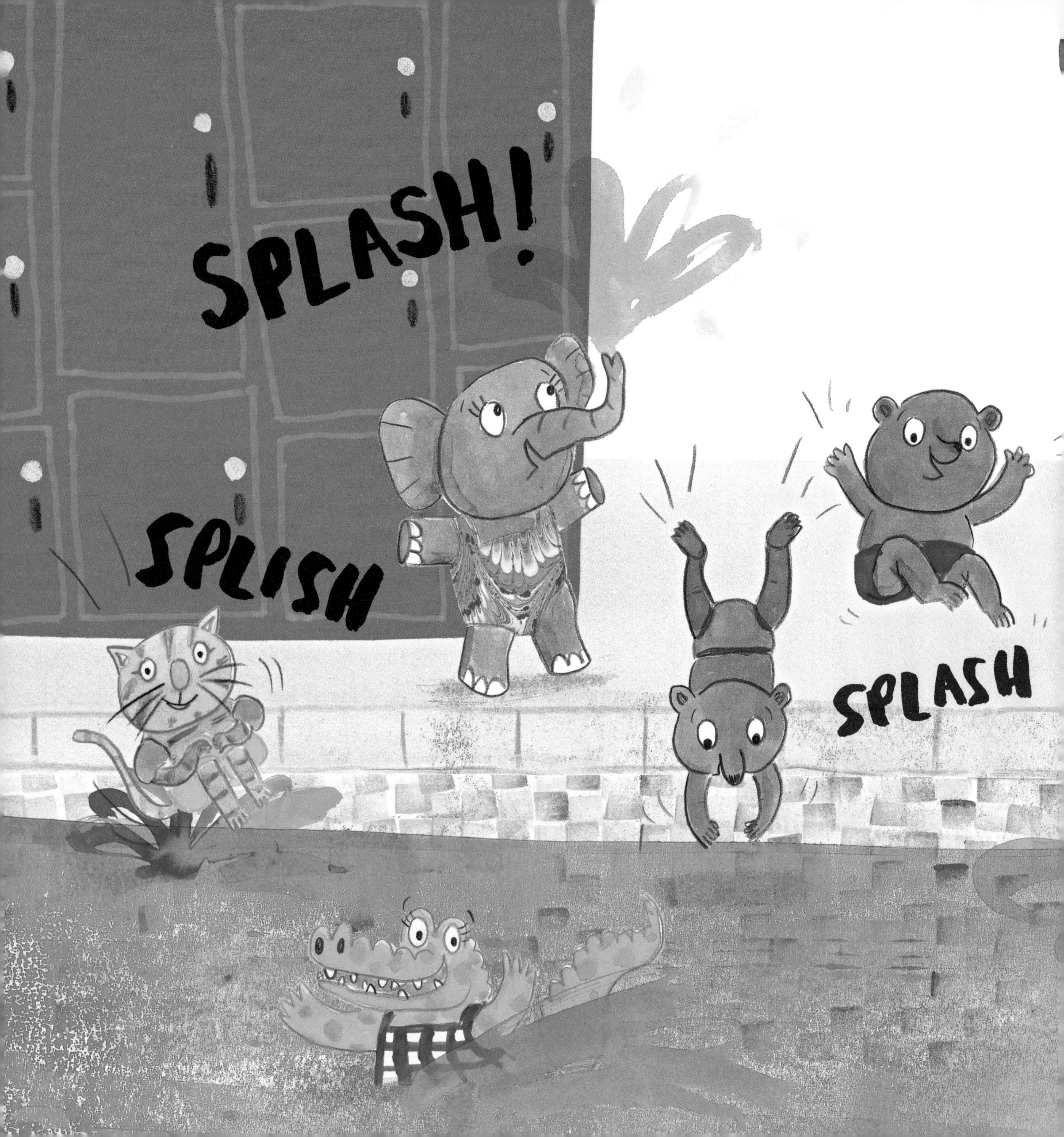
SPLASH!
SPLISH
SPLASH

Everyone jumped in!

But Eric just sat on the side.

SPLOSH

"Why don't you pretend you're a dolphin,
or a seal, or a shark, or a turtle?" said Flora.
"They're all GREAT at swimming!"

But this time the idea of pretending to be
something else **didn't** make Eric feel braver.

He dipped one toe in the water, then he heard Flora say,
"You can do it, Eric!"

So he took a **very** deep, **brave** breath and . . .

SPLASH!

…He was **in** the **water**.
And he felt **VERY** proud of himself!

Until…

... Sam **slipped** in a **puddle** ...

and **knocked** Desmond ...

Raymond **bounced** on Betty ...

... who accidentally **pushed** Raymond in!

Wo-o-o-o-o-o-a-a-a-a-a-h!!!

...who **fell** backwards into the boat!

Susie went **soaring** through the air...

POP!

...and everybody went quiet.

But something **amazing** was happening . . .

"LOOK, Flora!" cried Eric.
"I'm swimming . . . ALL BY MYSELF!"
Eric had never felt braver in his life!

But Flora didn't answer because Flora was standing
at the top of a very, very, very tall slide
looking very, very, very worried.

Luckily Eric knew just what to do.

"Why don't we **pretend** to
be **penguins**?" he said.
"They're **very** good at sliding."

Flora smiled, "You know what, Eric?
I think that is a **very**, **very** good idea!"

So after a few **very** deep, **very brave** breaths, Flora and Eric held hands, counted to three

1
2
3

and . . .

...They made it **all** the way to the bottom TOGETHER!
"Because best friends are **always** there
when you need them," smiled Eric.